ANGELO

the Naughty One

ANGELO
the Naughty One

Story by Helen Garrett

Pictures by Leo Politi

The Viking Press · New York

First published September 1944

Eleventh printing December 1969

To
Caroline Pratt

ON the steep side of a tall mountain in Mexico there was once a lovely little city. The houses were snowy white with red roofs, and the tall church towers were a soft rosy pink. Tiny stone streets ran here and there, and up and down, and around about among the houses.

All the little boys and girls in the city, but one, thought it was the best city in the world because it was on a mountain. This one was Angelo. He didn't like the city. He didn't like it at all because there was too much water in it. There was too much water in the pipes, too much water in the fountains, and even too much water running downhill beside the streets.

For Angelo, the naughty one, was *afraid* of water. He was *terribly* afraid of it! And he was afraid of it because he hated baths. He hated baths worse than anything else in the world! He just HATED them! That's all.

With so much water in the city Mama often caught him and scrubbed him. Angelo made such an outcry when this happened that all the neighbors shook their heads and exclaimed, "Listen to Angelo, the naughty one. What a terrible noise he is making."

Angelo was crying, "Help. Help. . . . Don't hurt me. Please. Please. . . . Let me go. . . . Ow! Ow! Ow! Stop! Stop! Please let me go. I'll never get dirty again."

As soon as Angelo was clean and his mother let go of him he would dash out of sight and Mama wouldn't see him again all day. When he came home at night he was just as dirty as ever. For Angelo loved to play

8

in ditches and in the mud. He liked to get down on his hands and knees and play with his little tin soldiers in the garden.

Papa said he was a disgrace to the family and Mama was ashamed, but Angelo was always naughty. He even yelled when his face was washed!

One day Maria Rosa, the eldest, was to be married. She was to be married at the church at three o'clock and nobody could find Angelo.

Angelo, the naughty one, had to have a bath.

Every other child was bathed and ready for the wedding. They were pretty and clean, and Mama was proud of them.

They all called together, as loud as they could—

"Angelo!"

"ANGELO!"

"AN...GELO...O...O!"

"Where ARE you, Angelo?"

But there was no answer.

Angelo, the naughty one, could hear them calling. He was hiding under a bush, a thick dark shady bush.

He had his little tin soldiers to play with because he LOVED soldiers *almost* as much as he HATED baths.

When he was big he was going to join the army and then nobody in the WORLD could make him take a bath!

Let them call as much as they liked—

"Angelo!"

"Angelo!"

"Angelo, where ARE you?"

But suddenly Miguel, the tiny one, poked his head under the bush and saw him.

"Here he is. Here's Angelo," called Miguel.

"Come out," shouted Gloria, the rough one.

"You must have a bath like the rest of us," cried out Juanita, commanding.

Angelo grabbed up his soldiers and ran for his life!

Maria Rosa could be married!

The rest could be bathed!

But never Angelo, the naughty one!

He dashed across the yard, through the gate and disappeared.

The brothers and sisters ran to the gate, too.

But all they saw was a herd of dainty goats tripping downhill to the market.

And two sleepy donkeys climbing uphill under eNORmous loads of cornstalks.

Only their little white noses and big ears showed.

Angelo was gone!

"Angelo shall not go to the wedding or have anything good to eat," said Mama, looking sad.

She gave each one of her other sweet pretty children a kiss and a cookie and said, "Keep clean till it is time to go to the wedding."

Then she went inside.

14

The good little children played quiet games and sang and laughed and kept clean.

They were *very* happy because they were going to the wedding of Maria Rosa, the eldest one.

But Angelo was *so* afraid he would have to take a bath that he ran

and ran

and ran.

He ran past the fountain where the family came for water.

He ran past the laundry where the women washed their clothes.

He ran past the church with the tall pink towers.

He ran through the midst of the busy market.

And he ran

and he ran

and he ran.

He ran out of the gates of the city onto the big highway. He saw an old man sitting under a tree. The

man called out, "Where are you going, naughty one?"

Angelo ran past him as fast as he could run and around a bend in the road.

There in front of him was a fort where soldiers lived.

This would be a good place, a safe place to stop.

He dashed up the slope and stood panting in front of the soldiers.

"Who are you?" asked a soldier, looking under Angelo's big sombrero into his dark face.

"I am Angelo," said the naughty one.

"Which Angelo?" asked another soldier.

"I am the Angelo who lives in the city," replied the naughty one.

"But there are twenty Angelos in the city," said the first soldier.

Angelo looked at the ground and said nothing, because he was ashamed to say to the soldiers that he was called Angelo, the naughty one.

One old soldier looked at him and said, "You are so dirty we cannot see which Angelo you are."

"We will give you a bath to find out," said a fat jolly soldier.

A bath!

Angelo gave a loud cry and sprang away from them.

The soldiers wanted to give him a bath!

Help! Help!

He started to run again but a long-legged soldier
gave a spring or two and grabbed him by the back of
his shirt.

Angelo was terrified.

Quickly he wriggled out of his shirt and got free.

But the tall thin soldier had long long arms and
reached out and caught him by his trousers.

Then poor little Angelo began to cry.

The tears ran down his cheeks and down his chest and left streaks on his face and body.

"Look," said the old soldier, "he looks like a tiger. We will call him Angelo the Tiger."

"Come, Tiger," said the fat soldier. "We will make you so clean even your mother won't know you."

When Angelo heard this he wriggled and strained and pulled and jerked.

But the soldier held him tight.

A young boy soldier ran and found a tub.

While he filled it with water Angelo fought like a real tiger. He hit and kicked, and scratched and bit, because he was *terribly* afraid of water.

All the soldiers except the young boy soldier and the big jolly soldier shook their heads at such a naughty boy and went off to look at the people going by on the road.

When the tub was full of good clean water the big soldier lifted Angelo up and put him into the tub.

22

Angelo sat down in the water and wailed like a baby pig being carried to market.

The young soldier began to scrub.

He used a lot of soap and he washed Angelo so hard that the dirt came off—and off—and off.

The big jolly soldier washed his hair and the young boy soldier washed the soles of his feet.

They washed behind his ears, and again and again they washed his face.

"What's this?" cried the funny fat soldier. "What have we here, under all this dirt?"

"I've begun to think it might be a little boy," said the boy soldier. "At first I thought we were going to find a real tiger. Then I was afraid it would be nothing at all, that it would just wash away and all we would have left would be some muddy water, a dirty suit of clothes and a very fine new sombrero."

Just then a fine looking young soldier came out.

"What are you doing?" he cried out in surprise.

24

"We have just found a little boy," they replied. "Maybe you can tell us who it is."

The tall handsome soldier looked at Angelo and said, "That is Maria Rosa's little brother, Angelo Silva. Why isn't he at home with his family getting ready for the wedding?"

Angelo, the naughty one, hugged his knees and sat very still in the water.

Since he had had a bath and was still alive he wished very much to go to the wedding and get the good things to eat.

But he was afraid of the soldiers.

"Now he is so clean," the fat soldier said, "what shall we do with him? We can't put him back into his dirty clothes again."

"I can get him some of my little brother's clothes," said the boy soldier, and he ran off down the hillside to his home below.

The jolly soldier dried Angelo's hair till it stood on

26

end and he rubbed his face till it shone. The young soldier came running up the hill with a clean white suit that was just the right size.

The handsome soldier said, "I will take Angelo to the wedding."

He went behind the fort and brought out a pranc-
ing black stallion.

He swung himself up into the saddle and the fat soldier lifted Angelo up behind him.

"Hold on tight," said the handsome soldier, "because this is a very gay horse."

Angelo was too excited to say anything but he held
on very tight.

The other soldiers came to say "Good luck!" to the handsome one who was going to be married, and they shouted with surprise when they saw Angelo.

"Where is the little Tiger?" they cried out.

"He ran off into the woods where he belongs," said the boy soldier, "and I don't think he is ever coming back again."

"Tigers don't like baths," said the jolly soldier, "but little boys don't mind them."

"Brother soldiers," said the handsome soldier, "sitting behind me on my horse is Angelo Silva, the younger brother of my bride, Maria Rosa. After the wedding he will be younger brother to a soldier and I am sure he will be proud and happy to take baths so that he won't disgrace the army. Good-by. We're off to the wedding!"

Meanwhile Papa and Mama and Maria Rosa and all the younger brothers and sisters were coming down the street to the church.

"Where is Angelo?" demanded Papa.

"I do not know," replied Mama.

"He ran away," shouted all the others together.

"He was afraid to take a bath," explained Mama.

"He is a disgrace to the family," Papa said. "He shall not have any of the good food at the wedding party."

"No," said Mama. "He will have to go to bed without any supper, the naughty one." But there were tears in Mama's eyes because she loved Angelo very much.

Angelo's family came down the street like a parade and Maria Rosa's friends came down behind them. On the steps of the church Papa and Mama stopped, with all their children lined up beside them. There was —

Maria Rosa, the eldest, who was to marry the soldier, and

Gloria, the rough one,

Juanita, the sweet one, and

Louisa, the bright quick one.

Next was Angelo's place in the family, but he had run away and brought disgrace to them all. What a naughty, naughty boy!

But sturdy Thomas was there, and

Little Miguel, and

Antonio, the baby, whom everybody loved.

That was the whole family. Their faces shone, their black hair glistened, and they all had on their best clothes.

Just then the handsome soldier came riding into the big square in front of the church on his shiny black stallion. Behind him came his friends, and most of them came on horseback, too. They looked very fine, riding into the square with their broad sombreros and embroidered jackets.

A little boy, all crisp and white, slipped down off the back of the shiny black horse.

"That looks like Angelo," Papa said to Mama.

"Oh, no," replied Mama to Papa, "that little boy couldn't possibly be Angelo because he is a nice, clean, pretty little boy. Angelo is a dirty disgraceful ragamuffin, not fit to come to a wedding. You would be ashamed to see him."

"But it looks like Angelo's sombrero to me," declared Papa. "It looks *exactly* like the sombrero I bought for him in the market last Sunday."

Then the clock in the church tower struck three and that was the hour for the wedding.

"Come children," said Mama, and she and Papa led the way into the great door of the church. Behind them came the children and the friends of the family. Next came the handsome soldier and his fine friends in their jackets embroidered with silver.

Once Mama turned her eyes to see if all the children were standing quietly as they should and WHAT did she see? She saw Angelo! Angelo! He was as clean and shiny as an angel.

36

Mama's heart nearly burst with pride because he was her eldest son, and there he was just when she wanted him most, and looking as fine and pretty as the other children.

After the wedding such a feast!

Such good food and such gay music!

All the neighbors and all the friends came to the party. They ate and drank as much as they wished, and they sang and danced to the music.

Right in the middle of it, enjoying himself most of all was—

Angelo.

No longer the Naughty One. No longer the Tiger.

But Angelo, the Pride of the Family!

And that is the end of the story of Angelo, the naughty one, who hated baths. After the wedding he was too proud to be *even a little bit* afraid of water. He scrubbed himself so well that Mama said that he could bathe himself and Papa looked at him and said:

"From now on I shall call you Angelo, the Brave
One, because you are no longer afraid of water."

40